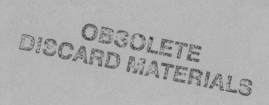

Journey in a Shell

Distributed to schools and libraries
in Canada by
SAUNDERS BOOK CO.
Box 308
Collingwood, Ontario, Canada L9Y 3Z7
(800) 461-9120

ISBN 089565-752-X
Library of Congress Cataloging-in-Publication Data
available upon request

Journey in a Shell

author: Christiane Renauld
illustrator: Corderoc'h

The Child's World
Mankato, Minnesota

Martin has never seen the ocean. He always goes to the country for his vacation, to Grandpa and Grandma's farm.

There are all sorts of animals there: hens, goats, sheep, and cows, of course. And then there are the pigs! As soon as you get near them, they start grunting.

Soon all of the animals join in the chorus.

Around the farm there are fields, woods and meadows.

Martin is familiar with all that. It's his own special country. All winter long he looks forward to getting back there.

Martin has never seen the ocean. He has never even thought about it.

Then, one winter morning a package arrives, covered in stamps of all colors. It's a present from Uncle John.

Quick, off with the string, then the paper! There, nestling in the bottom of the box...

"My! What a pretty shell!" cries Mama.

Martin has seen shells at the fish-market. Gray ones, black ones, white ones or light brown ones. But this one...! How fantastic!

He strokes it with his fingertips. It's smooth and soft, like silk. What's this? In the hollow of the shell, there's a message from Uncle John.

"If you listen carefully, you will hear the sound of the ocean."

Uncle John said, "If you listen carefully." Martin puts
the shell close up to his ear. He holds his breath.
Then he hears, as if from very far away, a humming
sort of sound, faint at first, then growing louder and
louder until it fills up the whole shell and his whole
ear as well.

So the ocean **is** in there!

This morning, in school, Martin has not been able to
do his work well. He can't stop thinking about his
shell and the sound he has heard. Is it really the
sound of the ocean? How can he be sure? After all,
Martin has never seen the ocean.

At recess, Martin gets all of his friends together. Thomas, Matthew, and Jimmy have grandparents who live by the ocean, and Sabrina goes there every year. Martin starts asking them questions.

"The ocean is big, and it's blue," says Matthew.

"Huh! More like green," says Thomas.

"Or gray," puts in Jimmy, "It depends what the weather is like."

"Can you see where it ends?"

"Of course. You see the coast. In the evening there are lights dancing on the water."

"You must have seen a sunken city, because there's nothing opposite at all. It goes far, far away, as far as the sky."

"To the sky? Does it go upwards, then?"

"I don't think so," says Thomas, "More likely it's the sky that comes down. In the evening the sun falls into the ocean."

"What's it like on the edges?"

"There's sand. You can make castles."

"What keeps the ocean in place? Doesn't it ever spill over?"

"No."

"Oh, yes it does!" objects Sabrina, "Sometimes it covers everything up. There's only a tiny bit of beach left. Then it stops, and goes away again."

"Where to?"

"I don't know. Maybe there's a hole in the middle."

"What about the fish? Have you seen any?"

"Yes, but not many."

"Then where do all the fish come from that you see at the market?"

"Well — from boats."

"And shells? The ones this big, pink ones, all shiny, like the sun?"

They all looked at each other in astonishment. Matthew shakes his head, "There aren't any."

Martin's heart sinks. Suppose Uncle John had just been making fun of him?

"Is it warm?" he asks, in a small voice.

"Not very. But warm enough."

"Sometimes it's freezing cold, too, though." cries
Sabrina.

"Does it taste good?"

"No! It's salty; I had a cupful."

"A cupful? You drink it out of cups?"

Everyone bursts out laughing. Martin is completely
confused by this time.

Luckily their teacher has overheard everything they
have said, and in the afternoon she tells them all
about the ocean.

She talks about warm oceans where thousands of colorful fish and beautiful shellfish live, and about cold oceans and all the ice beyond.

She explains that the sun does not fall, but disappears at the horizon, where the sky and the ocean seem, but only seem, to meet.

She talks about the tides, and how the moon is like a big magnet that draws all liquid surfaces toward it.

"What about the ships? Does the moon attract ships, too? And seashells? Do magnets attract seashells?"

With his head on his arm, Martin has fallen asleep. He's dreaming that he's off on a big white ship, flying toward a big, round, pink moon, like the shell from Uncle John.

At four o'clock Martin is back home again. But
everything is different now, because there on his
desk is the pink mother-of-pearl shell and the sound
of the ocean. It's as if the whole world has come into
his room.

Now Martin realizes that there are thousands of
things to be discovered.

THE CHILD'S WORLD LIBRARY

A DAY AT HOME

A PAL FOR MARTIN

APARTMENT FOR RENT

CHARLOTTE AND LEO

THE CHILLY BEAR

THE CRYING CAT

THE HEN WITH THE WOODEN LEG

IF SOPHIE

JOURNEY IN A SHELL

KRUSTNKRUM!

THE LAZY BEAVER

LEONA DEVOURS BOOKS

THE LOVE AFFAIR OF MR. DING AND MRS. DONG

LULU AND THE ARTIST

THE MAGIC SHOES

THE NEXT BALCONY DOWN

OLD MR. BENNET'S CARROTS

THE RANGER SMOKES TOO MUCH

RIVER AT RISK

SCATTERBRAIN SAM

THE TALE OF THE KITE

TIM TIDIES UP

TOMORROW WILL BE A NICE DAY

THE TREE POACHERS